MW00935422

1

To my very own super mom, I'm beyond grateful for you. You've never let me down once and your strength is admirable to say the least. I hope some of your super powers have rubbed off on me throughout the years. Thanks for being my everything.

Mommy And Me

Every night before bed, my mommy reads me a story. And every night is a new adventure. Mom has a lot of things to do during the day, so at night it's just mommy and me.

But what people don't know is that my mom is a superhero that saves the world at night.

She's a pilot that delivers specially

made chocolate milk to stores.

And she even becomes a famous artist, who paints the moon and gives it time to dry before the sun even sets.

And when I'm sick, mom makes me her chicken and pizza soup. It isn't the greatest but I know she tries her hardest to make me happy at all times.

Some days, my mom goes to my school and teaches children with disabilities. She tells me that disabilities are small traits that make us different. But our mommies and daddies love us the same.

And early in the morning, mom goes into the jungles, feeding and rescuing homeless wild animals. Mom has a little secret though, she can actually talk to the animals!

She tells them to always love and be yourself, just like she tells me. And to remember that family comes first.

My mommy is the nicest person in the world.

When mommy's birthday comes around, it's hard to find a perfect gift for someone who has everything. So we bake her favorite cookies, just mommy and me!

Who needs a superhero when you have a mommy like mine!

Acknowledgements

"Eyes have not seen, nor ear heard, Nor have entered into the heart of man the things which God has prepared for those who love him"- 1 Corinthians 2:9.

If someone had told me 5 years ago that I would be an author today, I would have laughed. But I thank God first and foremost for allowing this to happen and for being the cornerstone in my life. To my parents, the coolest superheroes I know, thank you for always keeping me grounded and helping me right my wrongs. To my sister, my heart, thank you for teaching me it's okay to be myself and having faith in me. To my family, my friends, and my loved ones; thank you for being a huge ball of love, support, and affection at times when I needed it the most. To my team, thank you for making my first literature experience an unforgettable one. Here's to the first of many.

With love,

Ebony

About the Author:

Ebony Troncoso ia a 21 year old preschool teacher from the Bronx, NY. She is currently pursuing her degree in Early Childhood Education. She loves children and works diligently with the youth in her church. Ebony has always had a passion for writing and has fulfilled her dream of authoring a children's book. She looks forward to many more.

* ** * * * * * * * * * *
* * * * * * * * ** * * * * * * * *

About the Illustrator:

Tyquan Price was born and raised in Brooklyn, New York. Tyquan attended Brooklyn College where he received a Bachelors in Television and Radio. Tyquan is a self taught artist and has been drawing frin a very early age. He became fascinated with the illustrations of the books he grew up reading. In 2016 & 2017 he created digital art for The Recording Academy (theGrammys).

CPSIA information can be obtained
at www.ICGtesting.com
Printed in the USA
LVHW01n0245140218
566535LV00012B/99/P